A Note to Parents and Caregivers:

Read-it! Readers are for children who are just starting on the amazing road to reading. These beautiful books support both the acquisition of reading skills and the love of books.

 The PURPLE LEVEL presents basic topics and objects using high frequency words and simple language patterns.

 The RED LEVEL presents familiar topics using common words and repeating sentence patterns.

 The BLUE LEVEL presents new ideas using a larger vocabulary and varied sentence structure.

 The YELLOW LEVEL presents more challenging ideas, a broad vocabulary, and wide variety in sentence structure.

 The GREEN LEVEL presents more complex ideas, an extended vocabulary range, and expanded language structures.

 The ORANGE LEVEL presents a wide range of ideas and concepts using challenging vocabulary and complex language structures.

When sharing a book with your child, read in short stretches, pausing often to talk about the pictures. Have your child turn the pages and point to the pictures and familiar words. And be sure to reread favorite stories or parts of stories.

There is no right or wrong way to share books with children. Find time to read with your child, and pass on the legacy of literacy.

Adria F. Klein, Ph.D.
Professor Emeritus
California State University
San Bernardino, California

Editor: Christianne Jones
Page Production: Melissa Kes/Tracy Davies
Art Director: Keith Griffin
Managing Editor: Catherine Neitge
The illustrations in this book were done in watercolor.

Picture Window Books
5115 Excelsior Boulevard
Suite 232
Minneapolis, MN 55416
877-845-8392
www.picturewindowbooks.com

Printed in the United States of America.

Library of Congress Cataloging-in-Publication Data
Blackaby, Susan.
A place for Mike / by Susan Blackaby ; illustrated by Mernie Gallagher-Cole.
p. cm. — (Read-it! readers)
Summary: Easy-to-read text describes what Mike likes to do at his favorite place.
ISBN 1-4048-1012-9 (hardcover)
[1. Beaches—Fiction. 2. Play—Fiction.] I. Cole, Mernie Gallagher, ill. II. Title.
III. Series.

PZ7.B5318Pl 2004
[E]—dc22   2004019184

A Place for Mike

By Susan Blackaby

Illustrated by Mernie Gallagher-Cole

Special thanks to our advisers for their expertise:

Adria F. Klein, Ph.D.
Professor Emeritus, California State University
San Bernardino, California

Susan Kesselring, M.A.
Literacy Educator
Rosemount-Apple Valley-Eagan (Minnesota) School District

PICTURE WINDOW BOOKS
Minneapolis, Minnesota

Mike goes to his favorite place.

Where is Mike going?

5

Mike likes to dig.

Mike digs in the sand.

6

Mike likes to dig and
play in the sand.

Mike likes to swim.

Mike swims in the water.

Mike likes to swim and
play in the water.

Mike likes to fly kites.

12

13

Mike flies his kite above the grass.

Mike likes to fly his kite
and play on the grass.

Mike likes the sand, water, and grass.

Where is Mike?

Mike is at the beach!

Mike can dig, swim, and play
at the beach.

The beach is Mike's favorite place.

23

More *Read-it!* Readers

Bright pictures and fun stories help you practice your reading skills. Look for more books at your level.

Ann Plants a Garden by Susan Blackaby

Bess and Tess by Susan Blackaby

The Best Soccer Player by Susan Blackaby

Dan Gets Set by Susan Blackaby

Fishing Trip by Susan Blackaby

Jen Plays by Susan Blackaby

Mary's Art by Susan Blackaby

Moving Day by Susan Blackaby

Pat Picks Up by Susan Blackaby

A Place for Mike by Susan Blackaby

Wes Gets a Pet by Susan Blackaby

Winter Fun for Kat by Susan Blackaby

A Year of Fun by Susan Blackaby

Looking for a specific title or level? A complete list of *Read-it!* Readers is available on our Web site: *www.picturewindowbooks.com*